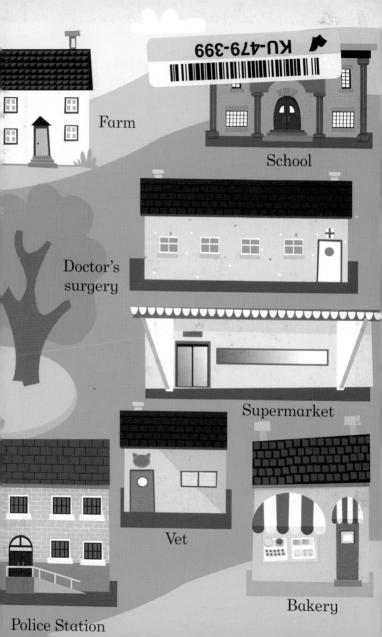

Farm

School

Doctor's surgery

Supermarket

Vet

Bakery

Police Station

A catalogue record for this book is available from the British Library
Published by Ladybird Books Ltd
80 Strand London WC2R ORL
A Penguin Company

1 3 5 7 9 10 8 6 4 2

© LADYBIRD BOOKS MMIX

ISBN: 978-1-40930-293-3

Printed in China

Just the Job
Ben the Builder

by Mandy Ross
illustrated by Paul Nicholls

Ben the builder woke up early one morning. "I've got to finish Mrs Dogsberry's house today," he said. "I hope she'll like it."

Ben whistled on his way to work.

"There's a lot to do before Mrs Dogsberry arrives," he said.

Ben whistled as he
mixed some mortar.
"There we go —
last few bricks,"
he said, laying
them straight.

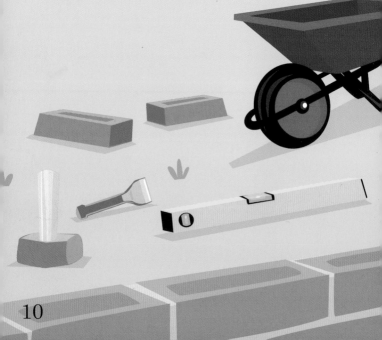

11

Ben whistled as he climbed
up his ladder.
"There we go — last few
roof tiles," he said,
holding on tight.

12

Ben whistled
as he opened
a pot of paint.

"There we go —
bright red front
door," he said,
trying not to drip.

Just as he finished,
Mrs Dogsberry arrived
with her dog, Barker.
Ben showed them around
the house.
"Perfect!" said
Mrs Dogsberry.
"But...

...what about Barker?"

"Don't worry," said Ben,

"I haven't forgotten
about him."

"Woof!" barked Barker.

19

"There's a lot more to do," said Ben the builder.

He whistled as he mixed some mortar and started building again.

"There we go – last few
bricks," said Ben.
"Last few roof tiles,
bright red front door..."

"Finished!" called Ben.
"There we go — your new
kennel, Barker!"
"Perfect," said
Mrs Dogsberry.
"Thank you
very much, Ben."

25

"Two more satisfied
customers," smiled
Ben, and he whistled
as he drove home
for his tea.
"I hope Mrs Dogsberry
and Barker sleep
well tonight,"
he thought.

And they did!

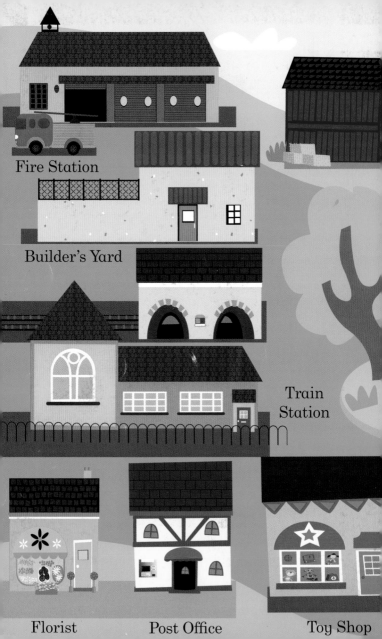

Fire Station

Builder's Yard

Train Station

Florist

Post Office

Toy Shop